ALADDIN AND THE WONDERFUL LAMP

For Deborah MacInnis

 Published by Scholastic Inc.
SCHOLASTIC HARDCOVER is a registered trademark of
Scholastic Inc., 730 Broadway, New York, NY 10003

Cataloging-in-Publication Data available.
Library of Congress number: 87-32322
ISBN: 0-590-41679-0

12 11 10 9 8 7 6 5 4 3 0 1 2 3 4/9
Printed in the U.S.A. 36
First Scholastic printing, October 1989

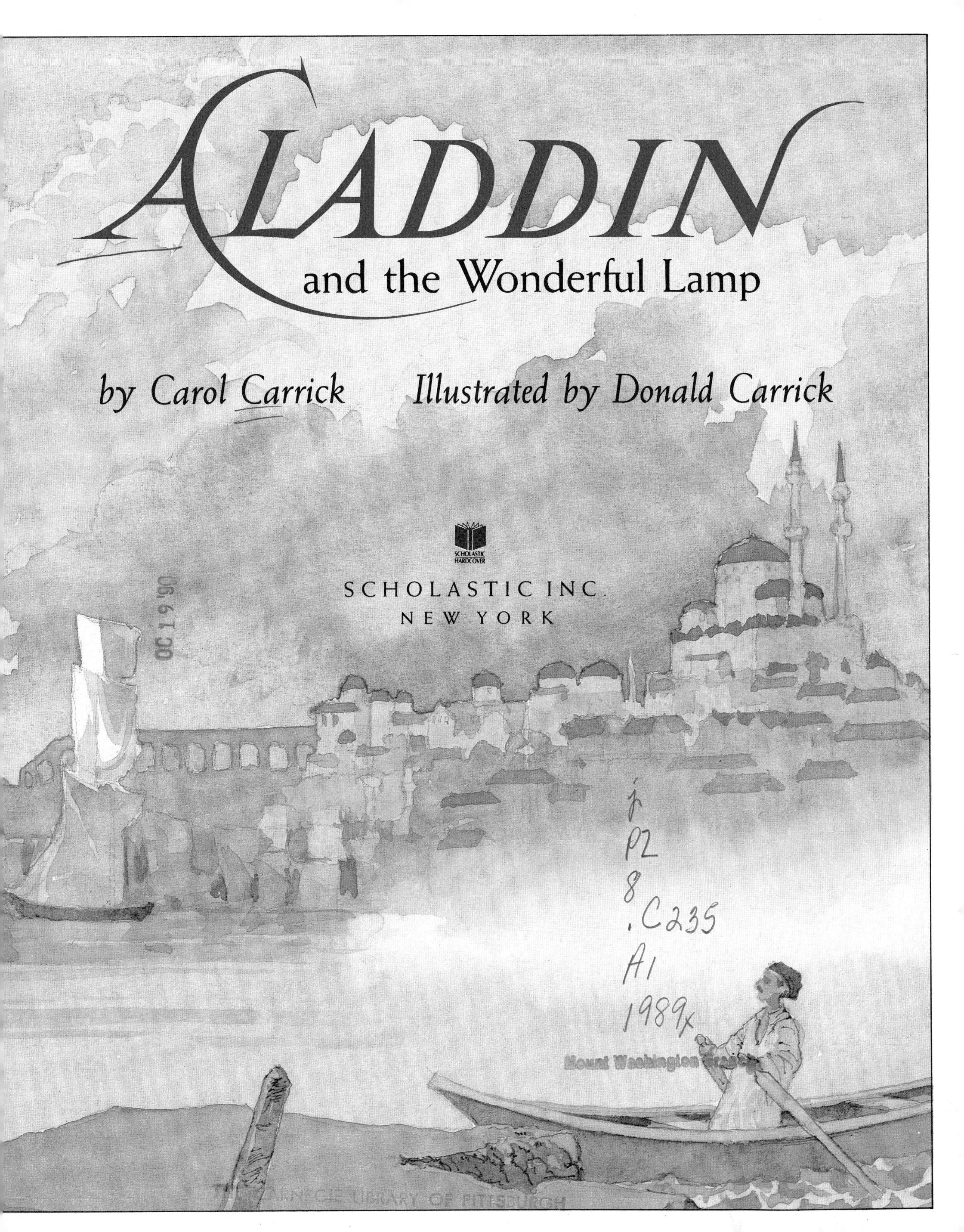

ALADDIN and the Wonderful Lamp

by Carol Carrick *Illustrated by Donald Carrick*

SCHOLASTIC HARDCOVER

SCHOLASTIC INC.
NEW YORK

THERE ONCE LIVED a boy named Aladdin, who spent his days in the streets of an ancient city. When his father died, Aladdin had no way to support himself or his mother.

At that time a magician came from Africa, looking for a boy he could use to make himself the most powerful man in the world. When the stranger saw Aladdin, he asked about him. Finding that Aladdin had no father, he said to the boy, "Are you the son of Mustapha the tailor?"

"Mustapha was my father," said Aladdin. "But he is no longer living."

To Aladdin's surprise, the man threw his arms around him. "I knew you at once," he lied. Then he began weeping. "To think I have searched the world for my dear brother only to find he is dead."

Aladdin was so happy to have an uncle that he brought the sly man home to his mother. But, of course, she had never heard of him.

"I have been gone for forty years," said the man, "and I've become rich. Let me take care of you for my dear brother's sake."

Aladdin's mother was grateful for his kindness.

The next morning, the magician bought Aladdin a beautiful suit of clothes and took him for a day outside the city. After hours of walking, Aladdin grew tired and wanted to go home. "Just a little farther," the magician said, "and I will show you something wonderful."

When they came to a secret valley, the magician asked Aladdin to gather wood for a fire. Then he threw a handful of incense on the blaze, calling out strange words.

At once, the ground rumbled and shook beneath them. It split open to reveal a flat stone with a brass ring in it.

Aladdin trembled with fear, seeing that this man was a magician. When he tried to run away, the man knocked him to the ground. "Take hold of the ring," the magician commanded him, "and help me pull up this stone."

The two of them heaved mightily at the stone until they had uncovered a staircase leading to a door.

"Beneath us lies a treasure that could be yours," said the magician, "but first do exactly as I say. Behind that door you will find a cave with three halls. They lead to a garden. Pass through them without stopping, and touch nothing in them," he warned, "or you will die. The garden wall holds a lamp. Pour out the wick and the oil and bring the lamp to me."

At the word "treasure," Aladdin forgot his fears and did what he was told. Sure enough, a glow beckoned to him from the back of the cave, and there was the garden of trees hung with fruit of every kind.

As soon as Aladdin found the lamp in the wall, he poured out the oil and tucked the lamp into his belt. On the way back, he was amazed to discover that the bright and colorful fruits on the trees were jewels. Forgetting the magician's warning, he stopped and picked some for his mother.

But the magician grew impatient. "Quick! Pass up the lamp," he called, for as soon as he had it, he planned to kill the boy.

"Help me up," said Aladdin, weighed down by the jewels.

"First give me the lamp!" the man ordered.

"As soon as I'm out," said Aladdin. "My hands are full."

At this, the magician flew into a rage and threw more incense on the fire. Instantly the stone slid back in place.

"Uncle! Don't leave me," cried Aladdin in terror. But the door to the cave slammed shut and he was trapped in the dark.

There was no way out. Aladdin fell on his knees to pray for help, but the lamp made him uncomfortable. In taking it from his belt, he accidently rubbed it. Suddenly sparks burst from the lamp. Aladdin dropped it, shielding his eyes from the light. When he looked again, an enormous genie stood in its brightness.

"What would you have?" The spirit's voice resounded from the walls. "I am the slave of the lamp and will obey you in all things."

The genie was frightening, but Aladdin was even more terrified of being left in the dark. "I want to go home," he pleaded. As soon as he said these words, Aladdin was at his own door.

The bewildered boy told his mother how the magician had left him to die and how he was rescued by the genie of the lamp. "But see what I have brought you," he said proudly, and he showed his mother the lamp and the jewels.

Aladdin's mother was fearful. "Put away the lamp," she warned, "and have nothing to do with magic."

So Aladdin hid the lamp away for many years. He was so glad that his life had been spared that from then on he studied hard and worked for his daily bread.

One day the Sultan gave out an order. Everyone was to stay at home with their shutters closed while his daughter went through the streets to the bathhouse. Curious to get a glimpse of the Princess without her veil, Aladdin hid himself behind the door of the bath. The moment he saw her he fell in love. From then on he could not eat or sleep unless the Princess would marry him.

Aladdin's mother knew that a princess would never have the son of a poor tailor, but she loved him and couldn't bear to see his unhappiness. One morning she wrapped the jeweled fruit in a cloth and went to the palace. The court was crowded with people wishing to ask favors of the Sultan, and Aladdin's mother could not get near him.

At last she was brought forward. "What business do you have with the Sultan?" asked his Grand Vizier.

The woman bowed low and shook with fear, for the Sultan was all powerful. "I beg you to pardon his boldness," she said, "but my son Aladdin has sent this gift. He asks in return to marry the Sultan's daughter."

In all his kingdom, the Sultan had never seen jewels so large and so brilliant, but he didn't want to lose his only daughter.

The Vizier whispered into the Sultan's ear, "Ask for more than anyone can give," for he wanted the Princess for his own.

"Good woman," said the Sultan, "I wish to know that your son can provide for a princess. Have him bring my daughter forty black servants and forty white servants each carrying a chest of jewels like these. Then I will permit them to marry."

Aladdin's mother was relieved. Now her son would give up his foolish dream of marrying the Princess. Instead, Aladdin called for the genie by rubbing the lamp. "Fit me out to greet the most lovely Princess in the East," he commanded.

Soon Aladdin was riding to the palace in splendor. Eighty servants, richly dressed, followed behind him, carrying chests filled with treasure. On either side, his servants threw coins of gold to the poor who lined the streets.

When the Sultan saw this sight, he wished Aladdin to marry his daughter at once. And the Princess was happy to marry this young man instead of the old Vizier.

"First," said Aladdin, "I will build a palace worthy of your daughter." Once again he called upon the genie, and next morning the city woke to find the most beautiful palace inside their gates.

When news of the wedding reached the magician in Africa, he flew into another rage. "That stubborn boy has discovered the lamp's secret. As I live," he vowed, "I'll get it back from him."

One day while Aladdin was away on a hunting trip, the magician disguised himself as a peddler and appeared below the palace windows, calling, "New lamps for old. New lamps for old."

Not knowing of the magician, the Princess sent down a servant to find out what he was selling.

The girl returned laughing. "That silly fellow says he will trade an old lamp for a new one."

Just as the magician hoped, the Princess laughed as well. "Trade him that old lamp of my husband's," she said.

The magician snatched the lamp from the serving girl and shoved it inside his robe. He hardly waited for the girl to select a new one before he rushed out of the city.

When Aladdin returned, the palace and everyone in it was gone. "This must be the work of the magician," he cried in despair, for without his bride he no longer wanted to live.

Aladdin spent the next years searching, and as he roamed, he saw how many suffered while others lived in splendor. His quest to find the Princess seemed endless. But just as he was about to give up all hope, he found the beautiful palace hidden in a desert. He sneaked in after dark and woke the Princess.

They tenderly embraced. "Quickly, tell me. Where is my lamp?" Aladdin whispered, seeing she was unharmed.

"The magician keeps it with him," said the Princess, who wept with joy to see her husband.

Carefully, while the magician slept, Aladdin slipped the lamp from under his pillow. "At once!" he commanded the genie. "Move the palace back home."

They sped through the night while the kingdoms of the world dreamed below them. There was only a slight bump as the genie set the palace down, but it woke the magician. Fearing Aladdin's anger, the magician fled to the house of a woman called Fatima who was famous for curing the sick. As soon as he was inside, the wicked man drew his dagger and killed her.

Once again the magician plotted to get the lamp. The next day he put on the holy woman's robe and veil and went to the palace.

The Princess was fooled by his disguise. While they sat together, the magician dressed as Fatima said, "How beautiful this room is. It needs but one thing... a roc's egg to hang from the ceiling." He knew that only the genie of the lamp could know where it was.

"What is a roc's egg?" asked the Princess.

"The roc," answered the magician, "is a huge bird that lives on the mountaintop."

The Princess went to Aladdin and asked if she might have a roc's egg. To make her happy, he called the genie of the lamp.

"What is your wish?" asked the genie.

"A roc's egg for the Princess to hang from the ceiling," said Aladdin.

"You shall be killed for this wish," the genie cried out. "And your palace burned to ashes," for the roc was the genie's master. But then he softened. "I know this was not your idea. It comes from the African magician. Right now he is in your palace disguised as Fatima. Take care, for he plans to kill you."

Aladdin pretended to be ill and sent for Fatima. When the magician bent over him, Aladdin saw the hidden dagger in the holy woman's sash. As they struggled, the magician fell upon his own knife and was killed.

With the evil magician gone, Aladdin and his wife lived in peace, for the years had done much to change him. From then on, he used the lamp wisely, and shared what he had with the poor.